Healing by the expression of love...

Wishing for Solace...

Nasir

Wishing for Solace...

Nasir

To someone I love...

Table of Contents

Prologue

There are many strange feelings that people go through. The feeling of love is something very special. It has many layers and forms and the way someone experiences love is only known to him or her.

Here is a collection of poems written to describe a strange form of love, where a person, even after being hurt, feels the love for someone. For them the love is not about winning someone but to care for someone without any comprehendible reason. These poems are also about taking rejection gracefully as, it was not about to get the person they want, but it was about selfless care and concern.

However, that person is still a human and that person's feelings also get hurt when they are being disrespected, ignored, and ridiculed. That person, even though they are in love, they retaliate for dignity and integrity, but are still concerned about the wellbeing of their love. These poems are a collection of strange feelings that a person is going through being pragmatic in love with someone.

1. Untold love…

Healer of my soul,
Like an elixir,
How to say,
What I feel for her?

I wish she be here,
Clasped in my arms,
Eternal is for her,
My love and my care,

I yearn to say,
But stops out of fear,
Perhaps purest is that love,
That's never told to dear…

This page is intentionally left blank for you to pen down your thoughts, feelings, and reflections...

2. Serene...

Serene but seethe,
And without despair...
How to say
What I saw in her?

She shrouds her pain,
With a smile on her face...
I want her to know,
That I truly care...

But I was afraid,
To be close to her,
If I would tell,
She would disappear...

This page is intentionally left blank for you to
pen down your thoughts, feelings, and reflections...

3. Charm…

There would be many,
Who would like to be with you…
You have got a charm,
And many would follow…

But Shall I tell you something?
That you feel and know…
I truly cared for you,
And I would always do…

This page is intentionally left blank for you to
pen down your thoughts, feelings, and reflections...

4. Wish...

I always wish,
I always wait,
To hear your voice,
To see your face,

Be clung on to you,
To see you romp,
To hold your hand,
To feel that warmth...

But how can I!
I am far from you...
I lost my edge,
And I lost you too...

This page is intentionally left blank for you to pen down your thoughts, feelings, and reflections...

Leaving me despaired,
you went away...
A lot is there,
Still to say...

I could have said,
Had you wished to listen,
I was deeply hurt,
And you had your way...

I still wish to say,
If you wish to listen,
That, still I wait,
And still, I care...

This page is intentionally left blank for you to
pen down your thoughts, feelings, and reflections...

5. Dream...

I had a dream,
I wished to fly,
And I got the wings,
To soar in the sky...

I spanned my wings,
beaming with hope...
Adrenaline rushed,
To touch the sky...

This page is intentionally left blank for you to pen down your thoughts, feelings, and reflections...

I flapped my wings,
Beats stood high...
And lo I was there,
High in the sky...

Up in the clouds,
I screamed with joy,
Exhaling all the fear,
I Had a big sigh...

Out of sudden,
I heard a cry,
Straight from my heart,
But I didn't know why!

This page is intentionally left blank for you to
pen down your thoughts, feelings, and reflections...

I asked that duffer,
What happen to you?
He caustically said,
Don't you know!

Look down the ground,
What is there?...
Broken dreams,
Everywhere...

What a shock! Such a reply...
Who is responsible, Am I!
And the duffer went silent...
God knows why!!!

This page is intentionally left blank for you to
pen down your thoughts, feelings, and reflections...

Perhaps! the silence meant yes,
So, it was "I"...
I broke down,
Oh, my desire to fly...

The shock was such,
I lost my flight...
I landed back,
And wished to cry...

I wished to regret,
With the heaving eyes...
I kissed my dream
And bid goodbye...

This page is intentionally left blank for you to
pen down your thoughts, feelings, and reflections...

6. Deep Cry...

I wish to smile,
With all the scars,
With all the pain,
You put me through...

With all the pain,
I am going through,
My heart cries,
But still loves you...

This page is intentionally left blank for you to pen down your thoughts, feelings, and reflections...

Ever I be alone he says,
She can't listen and feel that way,
Ever would she listen that cry,
She would feel the way I am dyeing,
Ever if I die this way,
I won't wish she suffer this hell...

Still, I live,
Still, I breath,
With all the pain,
You put me through,
With all the pain,
I am going through,
My Heart cries,
But still loves you...

This page is intentionally left blank for you to pen down your thoughts, feelings, and reflections...

7. Eyes...

Eyes are naive,
They can't hide,
What one feels,
Deep inside...

I have to live,
With the deep scars...
When Smile hide the pain,
the eyes say it all...

This page is intentionally left blank for you to
pen down your thoughts, feelings, and reflections...

8. Is it that easy!

They say it is easy,
Time heals the pain,
But it prickles inside,
Every now and then,

How can it heal,
After what was said,
Perhaps it would go,
When I am fully dead...

And I have to live
With all the pain,
And with a smile,
Whether sun shines or rain...

This page is intentionally left blank for you to
pen down your thoughts, feelings, and reflections...

9. Merely words…

No one can feel,
How it feels,
When you ask for the truth,
And you are lied to…

I accepted you,
The way you were,
But you lied to me,
Leaving me in despair,

You compared me,
Reduced me to nothing…
How would have you felt,
If you were compared…

This page is intentionally left blank for you to
pen down your thoughts, feelings, and reflections...

How would have you felt,
When for others,
I would have said,
You are nothing to me...

Friendship reflects in action,
And not merely in words...
When there was a need,
It didn't reflect indeed...

This page is intentionally left blank for you to
pen down your thoughts, feelings, and reflections...

10. Nothing to you...

I never had thought,
I would get,
Knowingly - unknowingly,
so close to you...

It's my problem,
it's my pain,
And I would deal
with this one too...

This page is intentionally left blank for you to
pen down your thoughts, feelings, and reflections...

After hearing -
"I am lucky,
That I have got,
A friend like you"...

The thing that hurts,
are your actions and your words,
That indeed meant,
I was nothing to you...

This page is intentionally left blank for you to
pen down your thoughts, feelings, and reflections...

11. Life is like this...

Why it hurts,
When disdained?
Just because you cared,
Even being in pain? ...

Didn't expect much,
Just a little...
To see a smile,
Was all my wish...

Did I expect
Any returns?
why would she care,
It's not her concern...

This page is intentionally left blank for you to
pen down your thoughts, feelings, and reflections...

But broken or hurt,
I can't cry,
I can't stop,
And I can't say Why...

Still wish you best,
Success and bliss...
This is life,
And it is like this...

This page is intentionally left blank for you to
pen down your thoughts, feelings, and reflections...

12. Perpetual care...

Deceit and sham,
Lie after Lie,
In the shrouds of truth,
All justified...

When reflects through the action,
What's concealed...
It hurts at a level,
That won't get healed...

But life goes on,
Whether bruised or healed...
It would have hurt less,
Had the words revealed...

This page is intentionally left blank for you to pen down your thoughts, feelings, and reflections...

just a bit of truth,
Was all my need...
I didn't yearn for much,
But lies did supersede...

I cared for you,
and I told you so...
I didn't have a reason,
and perhaps would always do...

This page is intentionally left blank for you to
pen down your thoughts, feelings, and reflections...

13. My chosen Path...

Now that I am a stranger,
After knowing for years,
Just because I love,
Just because I care...

You want me to go,
I would do this for you...
why blame me for things,
That I never do!

It pierced like a spear,
The words you have said...
It hurts at a level,
That I can't comprehend

This page is intentionally left blank for you to
pen down your thoughts, feelings, and reflections...

My suffering and my pain,
Kills me every day...
Deep in your love,
I went out of my way...

Let me be in pain,
I meant to be this way,
I have chosen this path,
Let me be astray...

This page is intentionally left blank for you to pen down your thoughts, feelings, and reflections...

14. It's up to you...

Now that you are among your people
People who make you smile and joy
May you always be in revelry...

But if the glare fades away
And you struggle to find a way
Think of someone,
whom you left behind...

Who never wished you to fail,
Who never wished you to fall,
Who never wanted to see you cry,
Who never wanted you to crawl...

This page is intentionally left blank for you to
pen down your thoughts, feelings, and reflections...

*Who tried to nurture
the wings you had...
Who always tried,
to make you fly*

*Who respected you,
the way you were
Who stood by you
with all the flair...*

*I wish you never
feel the need of me,
I wish you fly
and reach the sky
I wish if you have tears,
it would be of joy...*

This page is intentionally left blank for you to pen down your thoughts, feelings, and reflections...

But if the life
made you think of me...
You are welcome,
with respect and glee...

I never tried
to intrude in your life,
But stood with you
with all my might,
With small efforts
to make you smile,
You better decide

what's wrong or right...

This page is intentionally left blank for you to
pen down your thoughts, feelings, and reflections...

15. Just a pure love...

I would take time,
But I would recover,
Overcoming the trauma,
That I have suffered...

I was wrong,
I wished for solace,
And just a pure love,
And nothing else...

This page is intentionally left blank for you to
pen down your thoughts, feelings, and reflections...

This is an expression of many forms and layers of love. No matter how deep the love, care and affection are, a person's feeling does get hurt when ridiculed, humiliated, disrespected and lied to. However, love is such a strong feeling that even after going through hurtful experiences it continues to care for the loved ones... this collection is expression of mixed feelings that a person is going through when deeply in love with someone...

About the Author: Nasir works as a science teacher in middle east and this is his first published book. Born and brought up in India, He has got a bachelor's degree in science and is also interested in literature.